Due for Destruction

Written by John Parsons
Illustrated by Vasja Koman

Contents

Meet the Characters

Brooke

A volunteer at a dog shelter.

Karl

Brooke's father.

Dog 51

A dangerous dog housed at the dog shelter.

Dear Reader

I once adopted an abandoned dog. When she first came home, she was aggressive and had a lot of problems with her behaviour. I wondered if I'd done the right thing. But, with love and care, she slowly improved.

What happened to her? She's still here, sitting at my feet as I write this. Everyone, and everything, deserves a second chance, don't you think?

John Parsons, Author

A Cutaway View of the Dog Shelter

1. The office
2. The front door
3. The corridor of cages

1 Visiting Day

Gritty. Grimy. Grey. For three days, the relentless northwesterly had blown an air of irritation through the city. Brooke gazed out the grimy window of the bus. Grey concrete and steel, passing in a blur. She thought about her father, Karl.

The orange shirt. His orange shirt. Ever since she could remember, she'd always seen him in faded blue denim. And an orange shirt. Over the years, his face had gradually grown wearier and more lined and his eyes had become duller, somehow colder.

As the bleak years passed, the contrast between his face and the bright orange shirt grew stronger.

Brooke's thoughts were disrupted as the bus driver suddenly slammed on the brakes. Brooke lurched forward. Passengers jolted, annoyed, grumbling. It was the evening rush hour, and during this frustrating time of the day the journey from the prison to the dog shelter where she worked took three buses. Three buses – punctuated by twenty-minute waits between buses in rundown, graffitied neighbourhoods. There, even the fluorescent spray paint looked tired and fed up. Bus time. Time to reflect on the emptiness that the hustle and bustle of life on the other thirty days of each month disguised.

Visiting days. Always the same. The bus driver tentatively headed towards a set of traffic lights and Brooke returned to her thoughts.

At first, Brooke and her mother had studiously visited Karl every month, but her mother's willingness to visit the prison had drained away with the passing years. Now, Brooke visited alone. At least, she reflected, the days of the depressing bus journeys were almost over. Next month, her father would be released. Free.

There wasn't much conversation between Brooke and her father in the visiting room. With both of them living in vastly different worlds, there never seemed much to say, even though the two worlds were about to become one. For an hour each month, the small talk – the things people chatted about each day – seemed irrelevant. She'd asked him about his plans for next month, but he'd just shrugged. What plans could he make?

And, at the end of each visit, when she stepped back into the outside world, Brooke was filled with a mixture of relief and sadness.

The bus pulled up parallel to a set of double yellow lines. Only one more stop, thought Brooke. On days like this, she was glad she worked night shifts at the dog shelter. Once the day workers departed, there was no one else at the shelter. Unlike humans, the abandoned and stray dogs she worked with didn't chatter idly. And, Brooke thought with the first smile of the day, they were always pleased to see her. No matter how badly they had been treated in the past, their eyes and tails always seemed alive with hope and expectation the moment she walked down the corridor housing the cages.

The bus growled stubbornly through the traffic towards Brooke's destination. No passengers got on or off at the next stop. As the driver pulled away from the kerb, Brooke reached up and pulled the cord strung from the roof of the bus, and a buzzer sounded at the front of the vehicle. The driver slowed, negotiated a corner and swooped the lumbering vehicle in to the next bus stop.

Brooke waited for the automatic doors to open and took a deep breath to clear her head. It was time to rejoin the real world, a world of water bowls, cages and abandoned dogs. She stepped off the bus onto the pavement and, in the evening twilight, headed towards the shelter entrance.

2 The Red Tag

Empty. Unenthusiastic. Hollow. On visiting days, Brooke could hardly wait for the day workers at the shelter to go home. Struggling to communicate with her father left Brooke feeling drained, in no mood to laugh or joke with other people.

As the office door closed behind the last person to leave, Brooke breathed an audible sigh of relief. She locked the door carefully, pulled down the blind and headed for the dog cages. All the animals had been fed so her first responsibility was to ensure that water bowls were filled and to ascertain which cages needed cleaning. She walked down the corridor, inspecting the cages and their assorted inhabitants. At least, she reflected, they had simple, uncomplicated needs. Food. Water. Company.

"Hey, boy," murmured Brooke, as one of the abandoned dogs nuzzled its nose through the bars of its cage. None of the dogs had names. After three months at the shelter, dogs that couldn't be housed were destroyed. Nobody liked that aspect of the job – but the staff knew it would be even more difficult if they gave names to the dogs.

Brooke rubbed the dog's nose. Dog 12 was fortunate. It was a spaniel and she knew that it had a good chance of finding a new family. Spaniels were playful, friendly and cute. People liked spaniels.

She made her way down the corridor, occasionally unlocking a cage to replenish a water bowl or clean a floor. As she passed by, all the dogs greeted her with a wag of their tail or a gentle woof. All except one. Dog 51, the dog at the end of the corridor.

When Brooke noticed the ominous red tag wedged into the number plate on its cage door, she wasn't surprised. Dog 51 had been trouble from the first day it had been brought in. An ugly mongrel, aggressive and unfriendly, everyone had known that this dog never had a chance. No one would want it around. This abandoned dog was dangerous, unpredictable and troubled.

The red tag confirmed what Brooke and the others had known. Dog 51 was due for destruction. It had been living at the shelter for two months and the red tag meant there was only one month remaining.

The water bowl on Dog 51's floor had been upset so Brooke unlocked the cage. The dog was huddled sullenly at the rear of the enclosure. It didn't move a muscle at the sound of Brooke's keys, but its eyes flicked instantly in her direction and it let out a low, menacing growl.

"Lovely to see you, too," said Brooke, careful not to make eye contact. Aggressive dogs considered eye contact a challenge and there was no telling

how Dog 51 would behave if it was provoked. When it had first arrived, Dog 51 had to be restrained before anyone could enter its cage safely – but it had grown used to Brooke over the past eight weeks. Now it just watched sullenly and growled.

"I know you're not so bad," continued Brooke in an even voice while she filled the bowl. "With the experiences you've probably endured, you're entitled to be an old grump."

She backed out of the cage, always keeping a watchful eye on the growling dog. Its stubby tail thumped twice against the wall of the cage, but Brooke knew that a wagging tail wasn't always a positive sign. A low tail sweeping from side to side could be harmless or it could mean "be careful, I'm sizing you up". With Dog 51, it was difficult to tell – but wise to always think the worst.

Brooke locked the door and stepped back into the corridor. She had to remain confident while she was inside the cage, but she felt an overwhelming sense of relief when the door was safely locked once more. The red tag on the door meant her relief was tinged with sadness though. Nobody may have liked Dog 51 but, like all dogs, it would have been a lively, cuddly puppy once, until a life of neglect and hardship had changed everything.

Dog 51 growled at Brooke again.

"Maybe not so cuddly," murmured Brooke, as she turned and walked back towards the shelter office.

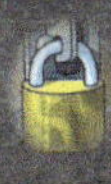

3 Paperwork

Suspicious. Unsure. Hesitant. Brooke knew exactly what the social worker quizzing her was thinking. "You know this situation won't be easy, don't you?" said the social worker, shuffling the papers on her desk and looking directly at Brooke.

"I understand the situation," replied Brooke. "But he's my father, he needs somewhere to stay, and I have a spare room at my apartment."

"Excellent," smiled the social worker. "If that's what you want, and your father agrees, I'll get the paperwork underway."

Brooke had little doubt her father would agree. What other choices did he realistically have? He wasn't welcome at her mother's anymore, and the chances of anyone else offering him a home were virtually non-existent. Being unemployed, recently released after ten years in prison and possessing a criminal record were not good attributes when you were searching for a room to rent.

"Good luck," said the social worker, closing the folder on her desk.

Outside, Brooke glanced at her watch. Five o'clock already. The appointment with the social worker had taken longer than expected and now she was running late. Brooke hurried to the nearest bus stop, fervently hoping that the buses from this part of town were quicker than the ones she usually caught to the dog shelter. She was relieved when she spotted a bus turn the corner almost immediately.

Three-quarters of an hour later, Brooke waved as the last of the day workers walked out the front door of the shelter. She unhooked the set of keys kept behind her desk and walked towards the door to lock it securely for the night.

She turned the key and was about to pull down the blind when she noticed a man in a suit and a young girl walking briskly towards the entrance to the shelter. The man waved and smiled hopefully. They looked like nice people. Not from her world.

"Can I help you?" asked Brooke, after unlocking the door again. "We're actually closed."

The man grimaced and looked at his watch. "Traffic," he said, shaking his head in frustration. "We made it here as fast as we could."

"I know how that feels," smiled Brooke.

"Look, I know it's late, but we're kind of desperate," explained the man, putting his arm around the girl's shoulders. "It's my daughter Bella's twelfth birthday tomorrow and I'm hoping you might have a dog that's good around kids. She's been dropping hints for weeks about what she'd like, and I just haven't had time to get to the shelter."

"Have you, Bella?" asked Brooke, winking at the girl, who nodded shyly. "Happy birthday."

Brooke thought for a second. It was late but, she thought, maybe not too late for one of the abandoned dogs. If there was a chance one of them could be rehoused, it would be a shame to send Bella and her father away empty handed.

"I'm just about to start my evening rounds," said Brooke. "Tag along. You might see a dog you like."

The man looked relieved. "Thank you," he said. "Geoffrey's the name, by the way."

"Brooke," said Brooke. "Come in, Bella. Follow me."

Brooke locked the door behind them and led the pair to the corridor of dog cages.

"Best behaviour, boys and girls," she called out. "One of you lucky animals might be going home tonight."

As Geoffrey and Bella walked along the row of cage doors, looking into each one, Brooke knew it wouldn't take them long to find what they were looking for. Tails wagged and tongues licked furiously in every cage – except, of course, for the last tail and tongue in the corridor. Finally Bella walked back and stopped in front of a cage.

"I like this one," she said. "What's its name?"

Brooke smiled. She'd been right. She'd known this dog would be fortunate.

"It can be whatever you'd like to call it," she replied. "Anything's got to be better than 'Dog 12'."

Bella waved to her father, who was still at the end of the corridor, staring nervously at Dog 51.

"Yes, I'd like this one," Bella nodded to Brooke.

"Excellent," smiled Brooke. "If that's what you want, and your father agrees, I'll get the paperwork underway."

4 An Unwelcome Surprise

Kind. Stable. Caring. Geoffrey and Bella were exactly the kind of people who would give Dog 12 the stable environment it needed.

After completing the checklist for dog adoptions and ensuring Geoffrey and Bella understood their new responsibilities, Brooke filled out the last of the forms they needed and closed the folder on her desk.

Dog 12 sat quietly next to Bella, its head on her lap, its brown eyes gazing up at hers.

"Thank you," said Geoffrey. "And thanks for staying open for us."

"No problem," said Brooke, standing up and clipping a new lead onto Dog 12's collar. "Good luck," she said, handing the lead to Bella.

"Thank you," said Bella, who could hardly take her eyes off Dog 12. This was the part of her job that made Brooke feel that it was all worthwhile.

When Geoffrey, Bella and Dog 12 departed, it was dark outside. The northwesterly had transformed itself into a bitterly cold breeze swirling around the alleyways to either side of the shelter, and the night was filled with the sounds of a restless city after dark. Somewhere nearby, a police siren wailed and, in the distance, Brooke could hear others joining in. After dark, this part of the city could feel threatening, but she had learned to take it in her stride. It was like dealing with Dog 51, she thought. Be confident, but always be on your guard. She locked the office door securely and pulled down the blind.

"And while I'm thinking about Dog 51, I'd better get back to inspecting the cages," she thought to herself. "There's water to check and cages to be cleaned." Completing the paperwork for Dog 12 meant that she'd fallen behind in her nightly routine, and she found herself late again. She headed out of the office towards the corridor of cages.

She walked down the corridor, checking the water bowls and cages. When she got to the red-stickered cage at the far end, she saw that Dog 51 had tipped its water bowl over again.

"You have to be more careful, buddy," she sighed, looking at the mongrel curled up in its usual spot at the back of the cage. "People might start to have suspicions that you're deliberately misbehaving."

Dog 51 twitched one disinterested eye and growled as if to say "who cares?"

As Brooke unlocked the cage door and stepped inside, the growling increased in ferocity and Dog 51's tail thumped repeatedly against the wall.

"Confident but aware," repeated Brooke to herself, as she righted the dog bowl and turned on the tap.

Suddenly, there was a loud knocking coming from the direction of the office. Brooke stood up. It was the door. Someone was knocking on the office door.

Brooke immediately thought of Geoffrey and Bella. She'd given them all the paperwork and advice they had needed. Had they forgotten something?

The knocking grew louder and more insistent. Brooke hoped there wasn't a problem with Dog 12, because having to take the spaniel back would be disappointing for everyone.

Brooke hurriedly turned off the tap and headed back down the corridor towards the office. She was running through the checklist of things she'd discussed with Geoffrey and Bella. When they'd left, everything had appeared fine. Why were they back so soon?

The knocking grew louder and louder.

"I'm coming," called Brooke, as she grabbed her keys and unlocked the door. She turned the doorknob. "I didn't expect to see you back ..."

CRASH!

The door swung open violently, pushing Brooke off balance. She tumbled against a nearby filing cabinet and twisted her arm painfully.

"Hey!" she protested. She looked up in shock and, to her alarm, saw that it wasn't Geoffrey and Bella who had been knocking, but a menacing-looking man with wild, hunted eyes who slammed the door behind himself. With a sickening burst of dread, Brooke remembered the police sirens she'd heard earlier. This man wasn't after an abandoned dog.

"Keep quiet and nothing will happen," warned the man threateningly. Brooke rubbed her twisted arm and nodded, trying to disguise her fear. She was afraid – very afraid – but, more than that, she was angry. Angry at herself, because she'd broken the most basic rule of all.

Be confident and aware.

She'd been one, but not the other, and now she found herself in real danger.

5 Keep Calm

Fear. Anger. Uncertainty. "Turn out the lights!" demanded the intruder. "I don't want the cops thinking there's anyone in here. Do it now!"

With her good arm, Brooke reached out until her trembling fingers found the light switch and the office was suddenly plunged into darkness. Outside, a police car raced up the street and its flashing blue lights filled the office with eerie shadows. Brooke's heart sank as the lights faded and she heard the car rapidly disappear around the next corner.

"Just keep quiet," repeated the man. "They'll give up searching soon."

Brooke shivered in the darkness. She sat with her back to the desk, her injured arm aching. Don't do anything stupid, she repeated to herself over and over again. Don't provoke him. Keep calm and appear confident.

The intruder paced up and down, pulling back the edge of the blind and peering outside every few seconds.

"What are they after you for?" asked Brooke.

"You don't want to know," sneered the man. "And I told you to keep quiet."

Brooke did as she was told. While she sat huddled in the darkness, wishing this awful nightmare was over, another police car accelerated noisily up the street outside and disappeared into the night. The intruder breathed heavily and pulled back the blinds to check what was happening outside. The sirens seemed to be moving into another neighbourhood.

Then, from somewhere in the darkness, there was a barely audible thump. The intruder whirled around angrily.

"I told you to be quiet," he hissed. "Don't you try anything stupid, lady, or you'll regret it."

"I didn't do anything!" implored Brooke. "I'm just sitting here like you told me."

There was another thump, and this time the man's reaction was even more menacing.

"I warned you, lady," he said. There was a chink of light as he checked outside once more, then with a rising feeling of panic, Brooke heard his heavy footsteps heading towards her.

"I didn't do anything," she insisted. "It wasn't me. I'm just ..."

And then there was a sound that made Brooke's blood run cold, a chilling sound that you never wanted to hear in a dog shelter. It was a sound that meant you'd crossed an invisible line from which there was no return. It was a deep, primeval growling and Brooke knew that once you heard that, an uncontrollably aggressive dog was about to launch a violent attack.

Brooke knew now what the thump was. She'd heard it just a few minutes ago. In the dog cage. On the wall. She covered her face with her hands, beyond anger now. With a flash of realisation, she remembered the blur of events that had led to her breaking the second most basic rule.

Always, always, check the cage doors.

She'd raced out to the office, expecting to see Geoffrey and Bella, but, in her haste, she'd forgotten to lock the cage door behind her. And the cage door she'd forgotten was not just any cage door.

It was Dog 51.

"Lady, I warned you!" shouted the man angrily. "Now you're going to regret ..."

With a furious volley of barks, Dog 51 unleashed its attack. There was a huge thud, followed by a crash, as the man toppled backwards under the impact of forty kilograms of angry dog thumping into his chest. Brooke sprang to her feet, desperate to reach the light switch.

Dog 51's volley of furious barking was deafening. She knew she had to reach the light switch before the crazed animal turned its aggression towards her. Finally, her desperate fingers found the switch.

The office was in chaos. Furniture lay overturned, files were scattered everywhere and in the middle of the floor lay the intruder. On top of him, straddled across his body, stood Dog 51. Its fangs were bared and saliva dripped from the folds of black skin curled around its lips.

The man pinned on the floor whimpered in terror. Frightened as she was, Brooke was relieved that the man was still alive. Dog 51 let out another chilling snarl.

Brooke edged back to her desk, never turning her back on Dog 51, and slowly picked up the phone and dialled the emergency number for the police.

She tried to stay calm, but, at the sound of her voice, Dog 51's smouldering eyes flicked instantly in her direction. It gave a low, rumbling growl and then, slowly and deliberately, it started to pad towards her.

6 The Doors Are Opened

Tension. Danger. Decision. Dog 51 stopped a few paces short of where Brooke stood with her back pressed against the wall. The emergency operator had assured her the police were only seconds away – but there was no telling what violence Dog 51 could unleash in those few short moments.

It growled again, but this time the tone of the growl was different. Brooke's eyes inadvertently flicked towards the dog's face and for a second she found herself staring directly at its black eyes.

To her amazement, Dog 51 sat.

"Hey, buddy," whispered Brooke nervously.

Thump. Dog 51's tail hit the floor.

Brooke was still wary. "Are you wagging or sizing me up?" she said.

Thump. This dog was impossible to read. Dog 51 twitched an eye and growled, as if to say "you figure it out". Then it stood up, turned

its back on Brooke and went back to guard the terrified intruder until the police arrived.

Brooke had been shaken by what had happened. She'd taken a week off to recover from her frightening ordeal. Even though she liked working at the dog shelter, she was nervous about going back – and especially about working the night shift alone. The shelter manager had immediately installed better security and given all the staff panic alarms to summon help immediately if they needed it, but it had taken all of Brooke's courage to catch the bus back to work after a week.

"I'll be fine," she reassured the manager, who was the last to leave on her first night back. "I just need to get my routine established again."

"OK," said the manager. "Good luck."

Brooke locked the door securely, pulled down the blind and keyed in the code for the new alarm. Then she headed for the corridor of cages.

"Hey, buddy," she said.

Thump. Dog 51's tail hit the wall.

"How are you doing?" continued Brooke. With a sinking heart, she looked at the red sticker which was still attached to the door to the cage. Someone had written something on it. Brooke bent down and read the scrawled writing. It was a date. Next week.

"That's too bad," she murmured sadly. She looked at Dog 51. "You rescued me. I know you're not so bad."

The rest of the night was quiet. It gave Brooke plenty of time to think and, as the hours wore on, she discovered she had plenty to think about.

The next day was a big day. Brooke hadn't really known how she'd feel when her father was released. She caught the three buses to the prison and waited where she was told. And then, when it happened, there was no fanfare, no fireworks. After ten long years, a door opened and there was Karl. Brooke's first emotion wasn't joy or relief, but awkward surprise. For the first time in as long as she could remember, he looked strange. He wasn't wearing an orange shirt.

Brooke and her father didn't talk much on the bus journey away from the prison. There wasn't much to say. The other people on the buses they caught chatted to each other about their daily lives.

"How was your day?"

"Where are you heading?"

"How's the family?"

Neither Karl nor Brooke had any answers to the usual questions people might ask each other. She'd told him about Dog 51 and her encounter with the intruder but other than that, they'd struggled to say more than a few words.

"My shift starts soon," said Brooke. "I'll drop you off at the apartment, make sure you're settled in. Then I have to go to work."

Karl nodded. He stared out the window at the grey concrete and steel landscape passing by.

"Two more stops," said Brooke. Karl nodded again, and then he cleared his throat.

"You want some company?"

Brooke looked at her father. Something in his tone told her that underneath his tough exterior, he was feeling nervous about spending his first night of freedom alone in a strange apartment.

"Sure," said Brooke, after a moment's thought. "I guess the manager will be OK with that."

Once the rest of the staff had left, Karl asked to see Dog 51. "I want to see this dangerous dog that you've been talking about."

"OK," said Brooke, uncertain of what her father really wanted. "I've got to do my rounds now, so just follow me."

"What's the red sticker for?" asked Karl when they reached the cage door. Cages made him feel uneasy.

Brooke explained that Dog 51 was due for destruction. "Thursday," she added. "I know it seems heartless, but it's the rules. Nobody wants to rehouse him, so ..."

"How much is he?" asked her father.

"He's free," replied Brooke. "He ..."

"Not yet he's not," said her father. "Open the door."

"Wait, Dad," Brooke said quietly. "He's an aggressive dog; dangerous and unpredictable. No one wants him."

"Open the door," repeated Karl.

Dog 51 rose to his feet the second he heard the click of the lock on his cage. His tail dropped down and his lips became tight. He stared at Karl. Classic aggressive behaviour.

"Don't look directly at him," said Brooke. "Aggressive dogs take that as a challenge."

Karl ignored her. He stepped into the cage, hardened his face, and eyed Dog 51.

For what seemed like an age, the two occupants of the cage stood motionless, eyeing each other up, no one knowing what would happen next.

There was a thump, the sound of tail on wall. Dog 51 sat. Then, in the middle of the cage, Karl sat. They both just sat there, looking at each other warily.

Brooke's father looked up at Brooke. "Haven't you got rounds to do?" he said gruffly.

"I can't leave you in here. I've got to lock the door."

"Then lock it," said Karl. "I'm used to it."

"I can't do that," said Brooke, shaking her head.

"Well, let us be then," said Karl. He turned his gaze back to Dog 51, whose black eyes were flicking between Brooke and her father.

Brooke knew she had no choice. She backed out of the cage.

Karl spent most of his first night of freedom in a cage. In a strange way, it offered him safety, security and familiarity. The difference was that circumstances had changed, and it was his choice. He propped himself up at one end of the enclosure, while Dog 51 huddled up against the back wall, as always. Nothing happened. Brooke went down to check on them every hour or so. Sometimes they were snoozing, sometimes they were just sitting there. Brooke spent the entire night feeling that this really wasn't what she'd expected. But the social worker had warned her that it wouldn't be easy and Brooke was finding out that she'd been right.

When dawn broke outside, Brooke headed down the corridor again.

"Dad," she whispered. "It's time to go home."

When Karl stretched, Dog 51's eyes flickered open and it gave a half-hearted growl.

"I'll have him," said Brooke's father.

"What?" said Brooke in disbelief.

"We understand each other," he shrugged, as if that was all that mattered.

7 No More Cages

Control. Behaviour. Fitting in. There were a million things that could go wrong. Brooke knew she couldn't face the challenge of looking after a dog like Dog 51 on her own. But maybe with her father there, things would be different.

Still, she was reluctant. She and Karl talked about Dog 51 until the first day worker arrived. By that time, Brooke realised that everything had changed. The separate worlds that she and her father had inhabited yesterday had disappeared and there was only one, new, unknown world now. And it included Dog 51.

"Second chance," said her father. "A new start. Who knows how he'll turn out?"

"They won't let us on the bus," said Brooke.

"So we'll walk," said Karl. For the first time in ten years, Brooke saw him smile. He pointed to himself and then to Dog 51. "Take a look at us, kid. Nobody's going to bother us," he observed wryly.

A new dawn. Sunlight, weak and pale. Old newspapers blowing by. Day one of a new world began by walking down a long, cracked pavement, past alleyways and derelict buildings covered in graffiti.

The northwesterly had gone, moved on to plague some other gritty, grimy and grey city. It was replaced by an awkward stillness, an expectant pause.

Brooke had no idea of where they were going. She didn't know what would happen and she didn't know how they would make it. But she did know that, for the first time in too many years, whatever happened was up to them.

She turned and looked a few paces behind her. Her father and a dog. It seemed strange seeing either of them on a street. For Karl and Dog 51, there was only one thing of which they could be sure. For today, at least, there were no more cages.

Grimy, gritty and grey as it was, this was still a better world than the old one. This one had a future.